GO NICK JR. DiEGO GO!

Diego's Springtime Fiesta

by Lara Bergen

illustrated by Brian Oesch

Simon Spotlight/Nick Jr.
New York   London   Toronto   Sydney

Based on the TV series *Go, Diego, Go!*™ as seen on Nick Jr.®

SIMON SPOTLIGHT
An imprint of Simon & Schuster Children's Publishing Division
1230 Avenue of the Americas, New York, New York 10020
Manufactured in the United States of America
First Edition
2 4 6 8 10 9 7 5 3 1
ISBN-13: 978-1-4169-4800-1
ISBN-10: 1-4169-4800-7

¡Hola! *Soy* Diego. I'm an Animal Rescuer. But today I'm getting the Animal Rescue Center ready for the big Springtime Fiesta! Do you like fiestas? Me too! I can't wait! I'm taking my Rescue Truck back to the Animal Rescue Center now. Come on!

¡Mira! Look! It's a mother cottontail rabbit. She has a big pile of cactus fruits for her family to eat at the Springtime Fiesta. How many does she have? Let's count. *Uno, dos, tres, cuatro, cinco.*

She has five cactus fruits! She must have five babies to feed. But where are her baby bunnies?

I see the rabbit's nest, which is lined with grass and soft fur. But it's empty. Oh, no! The baby bunnies are missing. Let's help Mommy Rabbit find them!

Don't worry, Mommy Rabbit. We'll help you find your bunnies!

My Field Journal tells me that rabbits leave their nests to go explore or look for food. Maybe the baby bunnies did that too!

Look! There are five trails in this tall grass. Do you think they were made by the baby bunnies? Let's go check it out!

A rabbit's fur helps it blend in with the grass, so we have to look carefully for the bunnies. Do you see a baby bunny in this tall grass?

¡Sí! There he is! We found you, Baby Bunny!

The baby bunny says that he was searching for leaves to decorate the Springtime Fiesta when he lost his way. We're glad we found you, Baby Bunny. The leaves you gathered are perfect for the party!

Rabbits love to eat grass and leaves on trees and bushes. Do you see any plants around here that a baby bunny might have nibbled? *¡Allí esta!* Over there! And there's the second baby bunny! She's stuck behind those branches!

Don't worry, Baby Bunny. We'll move those branches and get you out! The baby bunny says she was searching for yummy treats for the Springtime Fiesta when she got stuck. You're safe now, Baby Bunny.

My Field Journal tells me that rabbit tracks look like this. Do you see any rabbit tracks in this muddy riverbank? Which way did the baby bunny go?

¡Sí! The baby bunny went this way to the stream to get a cool drink. But look! He is stuck on a log that fell into the stream!

Don't worry, Baby Bunny. Rescue Pack can transform into a raft. Now we can paddle to you! *¡Al rescate!* To the rescue! We've got you, Baby Bunny.

We have saved three baby bunnies.
How many more do we need to find?
¡Sí! Two! Do you see another baby
bunny? There he is, under that log. He is being
very still. He must be hiding from something.

What is he hiding from? *¡Sí!* The gray hawk! Rabbits are afraid of hawks.

Let's be still like rabbits until the hawk flies away.

Uno, dos, tres, cuatro. We found four baby rabbits. But there is still one more trail to follow! Let's find the last bunny.

Do you see the fifth baby bunny? She fell into a hole and is too little to climb out. It's okay, Baby Bunny. We can pull you out! *¡Jalemos!* Let's pull! This baby bunny says she was practicing her hop for the Springtime Fiesta when she fell into the hole. We've got you now, Baby Bunny.

Let's count the bunnies to make sure they are all here. *Uno, dos, tres, cuatro, cinco.* All five baby bunnies are safe!

Now let's take them back to their mommy.

Mommy Rabbit is so happy to have her family together again! Let's all go to the Springtime Fiesta at the Animal Rescue Center. *¡Fantástico!* We can hop in my Rescue Truck to get there.

We made it to the Animal Rescue Center for the Springtime Fiesta—with our flowers and our new rabbit friends, too! *¡Misión cumplida!* Springtime mission complete!